PARADISE

Surprise party

PARADISE HOUSE

The Surprise party

HILARY McKAY

Illustrated by Tony Kenyon

**Hodder
Children's
Books**

a division of Hodder Headline

A Catalogue record for this book is
available from the British Library

ISBN 0 340 75301 3

Typeset by Avon Dataset Ltd, Bidford-on-Avon, Warks
Printed and bound in Great Britain by
The Guernsey Press Co. Ltd, Channel Isles

Hodder Children's Books
a division of Hodder Headline
338 Euston Road
London NW1 3BH

Chapter One

Four children lived at Paradise House. There was Nathan Amadi, and his baby sister Chloe, Anna Lee, and Danny O'Brian. Nathan, Anna and Danny were all nine years old. It was Danny who discovered the tent.

Paradise House was an old London house divided into flats. There was a big scruffy garden, which everyone shared. The tent was in the garden. It was hanging from the washing line on the first hot day of the year.

At first Danny did not even know it was a tent. It was cream-coloured canvas, faded in places. It hung as if it was very heavy. It looked enormous and complicated and somehow exciting.

Danny went closer. It had a lovely smell, grassy and canvassy and a little bit musty. He ducked under a layer of canvas so that it hung all round him and shut his eyes and breathed in very deeply. It's a tent, thought Danny. This is what is smells like, in a tent.

At that moment he was grabbed. The canvas was yanked away from his head, and there stood the Old Miss Kent. There were two Miss Kents at Paradise House, Old Miss Kent and Young Miss Kent. The Old Miss Kent seemed hardly ever to go out, but she was here now.

"Oh, it's you, Danny," she said, trying very hard not to sound annoyed.

"I was just looking," said Danny.

The Old Miss Kent stroked and smoothed the canvas as if anxious to make sure that it had not been hurt.

"It's a tent, isn't it?" asked Danny.

"Of course it is."

"Is it yours?"

"Yes," said the Old Miss Kent, making an effort to be friendly. "I am airing it. I air it every year."

Then Danny got himself into trouble. It would never have happened to Nathan. Nathan was clever. He would have known before he asked just how such a question would sound. It wouldn't have happened to Anna either, because Anna understood how people feel. Danny was not like that, he understood animals better than people, and he never thought before he spoke.

"Are you going camping?" asked Danny.

It sounded very cheeky but it was not meant to do. After all, Danny did not know that the Old Miss Kent had not been camping for nearly fifty years. He did not know how old she felt, or that she took care of her tent, not because she was going camping, but because she remembered going camping, a long time ago.

"*Are* you going camping?" he asked again, when she did not reply.

Then the Old Miss Kent's cheeks went red, high up under her eyes, and her hands shook on the canvas and she said, "You are very rude. Very rude. Very rude indeed."

Danny was utterly astonished. Also ashamed, though he did not quite know why. After that he was always extra-polite to the

Old Miss Kent, and she was extra-polite to him. Danny never told anyone about her tent. After a while he managed to put the memory way, way back to the part of his mind where he kept all the thoughts he would rather not think about.

The summer term at school came and went and the school holidays began. Old McDonald, the caretaker of Paradise House, began his enormous preparations for going to the seaside, and then he went to the seaside. Danny, Nathan and Anna did not.

"Next summer we will," their parents promised, but that was a whole year away, too far ahead to think about.

"You will have to make the best of London," said their parents, and took them out to parks and museums and the swimming pool as often as they could.

At first the best of London seemed not too bad at all. Then, three weeks into the holiday, it suddenly got very bad indeed.

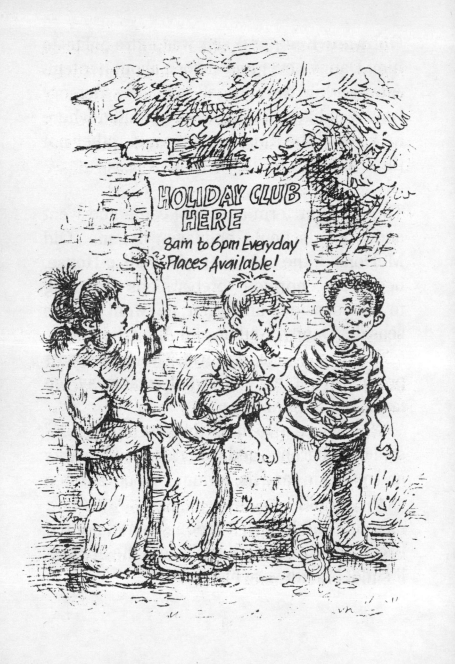

It was the sort of weather when it was hard not to quarrel. The air was thick and sticky with heat and the fumes from a million cars. It was the middle of August and the middle of a heatwave. Outside the school that the Paradise House children went to a large dusty notice sagged against the wall.

Holiday Club Here
8am to 6pm Every Day
Places Available!

Danny, Nathan and Anna, plodding home from the corner shop with lollies that melted faster than they could be eaten, looked quickly away.

"Bother my mum's new job!" said Anna as she tried to lick a trail of red juice that was running up to her elbow.

"Yes," agreed Danny, "and bother my gran! Fancy getting married at her age!" He took a large suck of lolly and the whole thing came off in his mouth and choked him.

"Bother my grandad too," said Nathan, gloomily gnawing off the wrong end of his ice-cream cone. "Fancy climbing ladders at *his* age!"

"Watch out!" said Anna suddenly, but it was too late. An avalanche of ice cream fell out of the bottom of Nathan's cone and landed on his trainer.

"Bother them all!" said Nathan, kicking savagely as it seeped into his laces.

The start of the trouble was Danny's gran who thoughtlessly arranged to have her honeymoon in the school summer holidays so that there was no one to look after Danny while his mother was at work. At first this did not matter at all. Anna's family lived in the flat below Danny and his mother, and Anna's mother offered to have Danny straight away.

"Thank you! Thank you!" said Danny's mum gratefully. "Anything to save him from You Know Where!"

You Know Where was the holiday club.

The second unexpected happening came

two weeks later. Anna's mother heard she had got the job in the local library that she had applied for weeks before.

"Starting Monday!" she exclaimed, half-delighted and half-horrified, but even before she had begun to worry what to do about Danny and Anna, Mrs Amadi, Nathan's mother, had offered to have them both.

"Nathan would never forgive me if I let them go to That Place!" she said.

That Place was the holiday club too.

Then the third and worst thing happened. Nathan's grandad climbed a ladder and broke his leg, and Nathan's mother said there was only one thing to do.

"Your father will be at home in the evenings and at night," she said. "He says he can manage with you if I take Chloe. I shall just have to go and stop with Grandad until he is back on his feet again."

"But what about me and Danny and Anna?" asked Nathan, as if he hadn't already guessed.

Suddenly the holiday club was no longer

You Know Where or That Place. It was Perfectly Nice and Probably Wonderful.

"It is terrible. *Everyone* knows it's terrible!" wailed Anna.

"It's *school*!" said Nathan

"Nobody goes," moaned Danny. "It's famous for nobody going!"

These arguments did no good at all. Anna's mother did not give up her new job. Danny's gran did not immediately come back from her holiday. Nathan's mother refused to let Nathan's grandad hop around his house as best he could. They said These Things Happen and There It Is and You Will Just Have To Make The Best Of It. It was only by the ice-cream money that the children could tell they were sorry at all. The ice-cream money was more than any of them had ever had before.

It was a Sunday afternoon and, although the traffic was humming in the background as it always was, Paradise House seemed very quiet when Anna and Nathan and Danny arrived back from the ice-cream shop. The boys went round to the outside tap to rinse themselves clean and throw water at each other, but Anna did not go with them. Instead she sat on the doorstep with her chin in her hands and sulked. The Young Miss Kent nearly fell over her when she came out of the door.

The Young Miss Kent was quite scared of children. It was brave of her to sit down beside Anna and ask, "Whatever is the matter?"

Anna was very pleased indeed to have a new person actually offering to listen to her grumbles. A little while later the Young Miss Kent knew all about the terrible holiday club where you worked all day even harder than at school, sitting in the same dusty classrooms or running round the same dusty playground that you had endured all year.

"Nobody goes," Anna told her. "Unless perhaps for a day, when they've been really bad and their parents send them for punishment. That happened to a friend of mine last year. For fighting her sister. At a wedding. They were bridesmaids."

"Oh dear!" said Miss Kent.

"But that was just for a day," said Anna. "We will have to go for weeks and weeks!"

"Weeks and weeks!" echoed Miss Kent sympathetically.

"It isn't fair!"

Usually when Anna said to a grown up "It isn't fair!" they got cross. They said things like "Lots of things aren't fair" or "You don't know how lucky you are!"

Miss Kent had never had children of her own. Perhaps that was why she was not very good at proper grown-up talk.

"No, it isn't fair at all!" she agreed.

Just hearing her say that made Anna feel better. She stopped complaining and sat quietly. Miss Kent did not get up and go indoors. She stayed with Anna and she seemed to be thinking. After a while she asked, "What would you like to do?"

Anna looked at her in surprise.

"Trips out?" asked Miss Kent, feeling quite daring.

"My mum took us on loads of trips out," said Anna. "Too hot!"

"Swimming?" asked Miss Kent, feeling very daring indeed.

"We did that with Nathan's mum," said Anna. "Too crowded."

"What then?"

"Nothing," said Anna after a long, long thought. "That's what I'd like to do. Nothing."

Miss Kent could understand that. She had done nothing herself, for years and years, and enjoyed it very much. She looked thoughtfully at Anna and an idea began to grow in her head. Even when Danny and Nathan, dripping wet from a water fight, came tearing round the corner of the house and fell over her legs, the idea still stayed there.

I could organise nothing, thought the Young Miss Kent.

That evening she told the Old Miss Kent about the terrible holiday club and Nathan's grandad and Anna's mother's new job and Danny's gran's holiday, and she added, "They are all out there now, in the entrance hall. I can hear them."

"Mmmmm," said the Old Miss Kent.

"No one had asked us to help."

"Of course not," said the Old Miss Kent, slightly shocked. "They know we are far too old."

Sometimes the Young Miss Kent woke up in the morning and thought, "Good Grief! I'm grown up!" On bad mornings she thought, "I'm old!" Never, ever, in her worst dreams had the Young Miss Kent thought, "Too old!"

Without another word she rushed out of the flat and into the entrance hall. There were Anna and Danny and Nathan, Danny's mum, both Anna's parents, Nathan's little sister Chloe, and Nathan's mother and father. They had all been talking very loudly but they stopped when Miss Kent appeared and into the silence she burst out, "I could look after the children! So that they did not have to go to that holiday club! I'm not too old!"

Mr Amadi, Nathan's father, recovered first from the shock.

"Of course you are not too old!" he said in

his deep laughing voice, and then there was a chorus of people agreeing that no, no, no, of course Miss Kent was not too old.

"But would you want to?" asked Nathan's mother practically.

"She offered." said Nathan, and Anna shouted, "Yes, she offered! Let her! Let her!"

"Anna!" said Anna's mother reprovingly. "Miss Kent you are very, very kind, but—"

"I'd rather be dead," announced Danny to no one in particular, "than go to that rotten holiday club all summer and sit in rotten classrooms cutting out rotten models and painting rotten pictures and putting on rotten boring plays. Anyway, she's not that old!"

"Danny!" said his mother angrily.

Danny looked at her in surprise and Anna came to his rescue.

"He was only saying 'Thank you,' " she said. "Weren't you, Danny?"

"Of course I was," said Danny, edging away from his mother and across to where Anna stood, holding Miss Kent's hand. "I think it's a brilliant idea! And this is the Young Miss Kent! She's nothing like as—"

. . . old as the other one, he was about to say, but luckily Nathan jumped on him just in time. They rolled on the floor together until Nathan's father pulled them apart, and then suddenly everyone was laughing and everything was agreed. The children would stay at Paradise House, doing nothing, and the Young Miss Kent would look after them while they did it.

Only Anna noticed when the Old Miss Kent came out of her door.

"But what about *our* plans?" asked the Old Miss Kent, but only Anna heard.

Chapter Two

One of the best things about Paradise House was the garden. It was not very interesting, but it was large, especially for a London garden. There was a wall round it, and a big tree that made some shade even on the hottest day, and a very tatty sloping lawn and a big rose bed. If there had not been a garden at Paradise House the children would never have been left with Miss Kent. They would have had to go to the holiday club. However, the garden made a safe place to play and Danny, Nathan and Anna promised to be unbelievably good, and the Young Miss Kent promised to say if they were not.

"You must, you know," Nathan's father told her.

"Of course, of course," agreed the Young Miss Kent solemnly, but secretly thinking nothing on earth would make her do such a thing.

She started looking after Danny and Nathan and Anna the very next morning. She did this by hovering happily in and out of the garden while they lay in the sun reading comics, and by not running away when Danny, who was animal-mad, offered to teach her a foolproof way of enticing worms up on to the lawn.

"Nothing could be easier," said Danny. "You pour a pool of water onto the ground and then you run round and round it. On your toes. With little stamps. And the worms think it's raining and they come whizzing up like magic. More or less like magic anyway!"

"How very clever!" said Miss Kent.

"I've been training the ones in this patch," Danny explained. "I've been doing them for days. Nathan and Anna used to help . . ."

Nathan and Anna stuck their fingers in their ears.

"... The more people the better, you see." Miss Kent looked suddenly apprehensive.

"Any age can do it," said Danny, remembering the conversation in the hall the

evening before, and suddenly Young Miss Kent found herself running round and round a puddle in her stocking feet, helping Danny to drum up worms. She was almost as pleased as he was when they began to appear.

"You are very good at it," said Danny, picking up a thin pink-and-purple monster and inspecting it carefully. "I'm sure I haven't seen this one before. I think it's new! Would you like to give it a name?"

Miss Kent thought very seriously about this. It was not often that she had a chance to name anything.

"Vienna," she said finally.

"That's nice," said Danny, putting Vienna back down on the grass. "Now we've got Tiger, Jake, Rover, Pluto and Vienna. I think they're getting to know their names. Stop laughing, Nathan!"

"How can they when they haven't any ears?" demanded Nathan, who was rolling around on the grass shrieking with laughter. "How can they get to know their names? They can't hear!"

Danny looked at him, and then down at Tiger, Jake, Rover, Pluto and Vienna. Nathan was right. They hadn't got ears.

"They can hear, Nathan dear!" said Miss Kent most unexpectedly, while Danny was still searching for an answer. "We know that is true, because they can hear rain. I expect they have ears we can't see. Like fish!"

"Yes, like fish," agreed Danny.

"Or birds!" said Miss Kent.

"Yes, or birds!"

"Or, or, or . . . snakes!"

"Crocodiles!"

"Camels!" said Miss Kent, getting quite carried away.

"Camels have ears!" Nathan told her sternly. "And humps!"

"Camels remind me of lunch," said Danny.

"It's the humps," said Miss Kent wisely, and hurried indoors.

"I knew I could cope!" she told the Old Miss

Kent as she collected sandwiches and drinks. "Would you like to come and see Vienna? Danny would be so pleased!"

"I don't think I know a Vienna," said the Old Miss Kent, and Anna, who had followed to help carry things, explained that Vienna was a worm.

"I think I shall stay here," said the Old Miss Kent immediately.

Anna understood exactly how she felt. "Danny has to have some animals though," she told Old Miss Kent when the Young Miss Kent had gone back out again. "And there aren't many here."

Old Miss Kent didn't seem to notice that Anna had spoken. "When we were children we spent the whole summer in the country," she said. "Every year, the whole summer . . ." She paused, obviously remembering long ago summers, and Anna waited. "The whole summer," repeated Old Miss Kent.

"Lovely," said Anna.

"Old Miss Kent," said Nathan, that afternoon, "is fed up. She doesn't like Young Miss Kent looking after us."

He was lying on his stomach, trying to set fire to his comic by focusing the sunshine through a scratched plastic magnifying glass.

"She was all right when I went to help wash up the lunch stuff," said Danny. "She let me wash up her special cup."

Danny and the Old Miss Kent were still being terribly polite to each other. When Danny, stiff with good manners, had turned from the kitchen sink and said to her, "Please, shall I wash your cup too?" the Old Miss Kent had replied, "Thank you, that would be very kind!"

She had handed it over just as if it was any ordinary piece of china, and not the pink-and-gold, curly-handled, egg-shell-thin, treasure of a cup, that no one else, not even the Young Miss Kent, had ever been allowed to touch.

"Oh dear, oh dear, oh dear!" the Young Miss Kent exclaimed, which alarmed Danny very much. All the time that he was washing and rinsing and drying the cup she had wrung her hands and moaned quietly and when it was safely back on the table again she gasped out loud with relief.

"What's so special about Old Miss Kent's cup?" Nathan asked Danny.

"It's old," Danny explained. "She's had it a long time. She's had it nearly *sixty years!* It will be sixty years, on Thursday, if no one smashes it before then. But she let me wash it."

"I still think she's fed up," said Nathan stubbornly. "This magnifying glass is never

going to make this comic catch fire. I need a
proper one."

"She's got one."

"Who? Old Miss Kent?"

"She was doing her crossword with it while
I was washing up. A big glass one, ten times
bigger than yours."

"Oh!" said Nathan longingly, and then,

"She'd never lend it to me."

"She might. She let me wash her cup. Ask and see!"

"No," said Nathan.

"Dare you," said Danny.

"I would be very, very careful," Nathan told the Old Miss Kent earnestly. "I just want to try it once. To see if it's true that it works."

"It *used* to work," said the Young Miss Kent doubtfully, as if sunlight might have changed since she last tried it.

"We used to burn our names," said the Old Miss Kent.

"What *was* your name?" asked Nathan.

"Emily," said the Old Miss Kent. "It still is Emily," she added, and handed him the glass.

Nathan burnt EMILY on the corner of his comic and took it in to show her and on the way, on the stone doorstep of Paradise House, he dropped the magnifying glass and it cracked right across. The Miss Kents, Old and Young, were aghast at his tears.

"It doesn't matter at all!" exclaimed the Young Miss Kent, nearly weeping herself. "Emily, tell him it doesn't matter at all!"

"It doesn't matter at all," repeated the Old Miss Kent obediently. "It was just a magnifying glass. It wasn't special!"

"Wasn't it?"

"Not in the least!"

"Not like your cup?"

"No, no, no," chorused the Miss Kents together.

"That was a birthday present," explained the Young Miss Kent. "She was ten, weren't you Emily, when she was given that cup . . ."

Old Miss Kent was bending over the scrap of paper with her name scorched on it in brown sun-letters.

"Emily," she murmured. "How it takes me back, just to see it! I wish these children could have seen our camps."

"Did you have camps?" asked Nathan enviously.

"Yes, yes," Young Miss Kent told him eagerly, delighted to see that his tears were over. "Every summer! In the damson orchard of the cottage. We used to call them the Birthday Camps..."

Old Miss Kent suddenly stood up and marched out of the room.

"She's going to be seventy on Thursday," whispered the Young Miss Kent. "And she doesn't like it!"

"Oh," said Nathan.

"And neither should I, if it was me," said Miss Kent. "But it's not," she added thankfully.

Nathan rushed outside and into the garden, leaping over Anna and Danny who were half-asleep on the lawn.

"She's having a birthday," he announced, jumping backwards and forwards over them until they woke up properly. "Old Miss Kent is! On Thursday. Seventy she'll be! We're going to make her a birthday party!"

"Does she want one?" asked Danny sleepily. "Did she ask us to?"

"Of course she didn't!"

"Did she like the magnifying-glass writing?" asked Anna.

"Yes . . ."

"Good!"

"But I broke it!"

"Nathan!"

"That's why we're doing the birthday party. To make up. And to cheer her up because she doesn't want to be seventy."

"Old Miss Kent," said Danny, "doesn't seem the party sort to me. I bet she'd hate a proper party. Chicken nuggets and pass-the-parcel—"

"Not that sort of party! interrupted Nathan scornfully.

"Old ladies have quiet parties," agreed Anna. "With little square sandwiches and no balloons and they have their hair done in those squashed sort of curls and drink tea."

"Not that sort either!" said Nathan. "Something she properly likes. Like when Danny went to the zoo on his birthday. Think of something she likes!"

"Crosswords?" suggested Anna doubtfully. "But I've never heard of a crossword party."

Danny said that a crossword party would be no good anyway, now that Nathan had smashed her magnifying glass . . .

"Danny!" exclaimed Anna reproachfully.

"What?" asked Danny. "What's the matter? I was going to say, I know what she does like. She likes her tent!"

"Her tent?" asked Anna wonderingly. "Has she a tent?"

"Yes. A big old-fashioned one. I've seen it."

"That's what we'll do then!" cried Nathan. "We'll make her a camp for her tent! They used to have birthday camps! We'll make it just like the ones they used to have and we'll keep it a secret and have it all ready for her birthday!"

"How can we make it exactly like it was and keep it a secret at the same time?" asked Danny. "How will we know what it was like?"

"We'll find things out without them noticing," said Nathan.

The first thing they found out nearly finished

off the plans before they began. Old McDonald, the caretaker, had put the Young Miss Kent in charge of watering the roses he had planted in the garden of Paradise House. Danny, Anna and Nathan volunteered to help the moment she appeared with the hosepipe and very shortly afterwards were all dripping wet.

"Comfortable at last!" said Anna, putting her finger over the end of the hose pipe and aiming straight upwards so that the water pattered down like rain.

"We were lucky," said Miss Kent, smiling at her. "We had the stream in weather like this."

"A stream?" asked Nathan.

"At the bottom of the orchard. It ran over a bed of white chalky stones."

"A proper stream with fish and things?"

"Oh yes! All sorts of creatures! And we used to dam it to make a pond . . ."

"A pond?"

"Of course we got very wet, but it was all part of summer . . . Look, look, a worm has come up to enjoy the water! Could it possibly be Vienna, Danny dear?"

Danny hurried over to check and became so engrossed that he forgot about birthday camps. Anna forgot as well, in the excitement of discovering that if she aimed the hosepipe into the sunlight she could make rainbows in the spray. Nathan was not so easily distracted. He paced around the garden murmuring,

"A stream and a pond! A stream and a pond ..."

Chapter Three

Nathan's mother and little sister Chloe were staying at Nathan's grandad's house, so it was his father who cooked supper and got him into bed that night.

"It's too hot to go to sleep," objected Nathan.

"It's too hot not to," said his father, but he pulled open both windows as far as they would go.

"Don't go yet!" begged Nathan. "Stay and talk! What do you think mum is doing right now?"

"You missing her?" asked his father and Nathan said Yes, and then No, and then Sometimes, and then he said, "Let's play Next Year."

Next Year was a game that Nathan and his father had played for years and years. It was a cheering-up game. Nathan's father, wondering a little what was wrong, sat down on the end of the bed.

"Next year," he said, beginning at once, "we'll buy at yacht . . . or a sailing ship?"

"A sailing ship," said Nathan, cheering up already.

"And we'll take a cruise, just you and me . . ."

"And Danny and Anna."

"And your mum and Chloe?"

"We'll leave Chloe with grandad. He'll be better by then."

"Possibly leaving Chloe with grandad . . ."

"We'll bring them back fantastic presents. Shells and parrots and wild coconuts and pearls . . ."

". . . Two palm trees and a hammock for your grandad . . ."

"Where shall we go first?" asked Nathan.

"Barbados."

"A long way."

"You can swim every day off the side of the ship."

"Sharks?"

"Bound to be. Sharks, dolphins, flying fish, whales, octopuses."

"Danny will tame them."

"That's what I thought."

"Dad?"

"Hmmm?"

"Could I have a Christmas present early?"

"I knew you were leading up to something!"

exclaimed his father. "I've been sitting here thinking 'Either he's missing his mum, or all this is leading up to something!' "

"I *do* miss Mum," protested Nathan. "And it's very quiet without Chloe. I keep expecting her to come crashing in!"

"Me too. What's this Christmas present then?"

"Only a paddling pool."

"Well, that won't break the bank," said his father, sighing with relief. "A paddling pool is what you need this weather! What about Danny and Anna?"

"Anna's got one somewhere she thinks. Danny's asking his mum tonight. Are there any uninhabited islands on the way to Barbados?"

"Only treasure ones."

Nathan sighed happily.

Danny said to his mother, "I think Nathan's getting a paddling pool."

"You'd better have one too," said Danny's mother.

Anna had a paddling pool. She fished it out from under her bed where it had been stuffed, still wet, two years before. It seemed to have glued itself into a tangle of plastic creases. Musty grass cuttings and dried mud fell off as

she tried to pull it into shape. She carted it into the bathroom and gave it a hot shower, hoping to soften it back into life.

"What *are* you doing?" demanded her mother, coming in to see what all the splashing was about and looking with disgust at the bath, now half-full of muddy water and dead floating grass.

"Sorting out my paddling pool," said Anna, tugging hard at a crease. A bit more sticky plastic peeled apart and a pair of mouldering socks bobbed to the surface.

"My Dalmatian socks!" said Anna, fishing them out.

"Put them in the bin at once!" ordered her mother. "In fact the whole thing ought to go into the bin! Just smell it! Take it outside, Anna, for goodness sake! If you want a paddling pool . . ."

"I do, I do! We're all having paddling pools! Nathan and Danny are getting new ones from the shop on the corner! Nathan said . . ."

"What?" asked her mother suspiciously.

"He said we should all have paddling pools," said Anna meekly.

"I'll get you one tomorrow," promised her mother.

"Three paddling pools!," said Nathan, very pleased, the next morning. "Spaced out they will make a brilliant stream. We'll sink them, each a bit lower than the one before with channels joining them made out of Anna's old one, cut up . . ."

"It's in the dustbin," said Anna.

"We'll get it out. We'll make a stream to run down the slope of the lawn. We'll use the hose-pipe to fill up the top pool and the water will run down, just like a real stream, and come out at the bottom. We'll put it so that it runs out into the roses, then no one can say it's a waste . . ."

There was nothing Nathan liked better than making things outdoors, and the more complicated and messy they were the more he liked them, but Danny and Anna were not so keen.

"It's going to take a terrible lot of digging," said Danny. "And the Young Miss Kent is bound to want to know what we're doing. What will we tell her?"

"We'll think of something," said Nathan airily.

"It's a good job Old McDonald isn't here!" said Anna.

"Yes, but he *isn't* here!" said Nathan impatiently. "Come on, let's go and borrow his spade!"

However, they could not begin at once. The Young Miss Kent appeared and offered her help with Danny's daily worm training session. This was done, and Tiger, Jake, Rover and Pluto came almost immediately, but no amount of pouring on water or running in circles could induce Vienna to appear.

Miss Kent was particularly disappointed.

"Don't worry," Nathan told her, suddenly inspired. "We'll find her for you!"

It was the perfect excuse and, to Miss Kent's astonishment, they dug all morning. Three large holes appeared across the lawn, but no worm that looked quite like Vienna.

"Really, you are working far too hard!" the Young Miss Kent protested at lunchtime. "I thought you wanted to do nothing!"

"We did that yesterday," said Anna. "Tell us some more about your camp."

"There isn't really much to tell, dear," said the Young Miss Kent, while her sister picked sadly at a minute portion of ham and salad. "We had the big tent, of course, that we slept in . . ."

"What did you do when it rained?"

"I don't think it ever rained. I don't think it ever rained once all summer!"

"Did you have sleeping bags?"

"No, no. Hay bags to lie down on, and blankets on top. We stuffed the hay bags ourselves. They smelt wonderful."

"Birds!" said the Old Miss Kent, suddenly joining in. "Birds everywhere! It's the birds I

think of most! The sound of their wings, and the sound of the water . . ."

Danny could hardly wait for lunch to be over. He loved birds, and his best Christmas present had been a birdtable that fastened to his bedroom windowsill.

"I've got all sorts coming," he told Nathan and Anna proudly. "Starlings and sparrows and jackdaws. Bluetits and chaffinches and sometimes a robin. They come to my bedroom, but I'm sure they'd come into the garden if we put out food for them there instead. And I might be able to get some hay to make hay bags as well!"

"How?" asked Anna.

"Wait and see," said Danny mysteriously.

The corner shop only sold one sort of paddling pool, small round ones with blue bottoms and clear sides patterned with weeds and fish.

"Perfect for stream-making!" said Nathan, when they began to arrive. His was the first, dropped off by his father in his lunch break.

Nathan and Anna began the difficult job of fitting it into its hole while Danny hurried to the pet shop down the road for birdseed.

Danny was allowed to go to the pet shop on his own. He often spent whole Saturday mornings there while his mum went shopping. He and the pet shop man were old friends. Even though Danny never bought anything much except goldfish food he dropped in constantly to check the latest arrivals, chat to William the parrot, and sweep the floor under the bird cages. One whole wall of the shop was entirely bird cages, and the floor beneath them was always crunchy with birdseed. Since Danny had got his own birdtable the pet shop man had saved all his swept-up birdseed for him. In return Danny helped with the never-ending job of bagging up hay.

For a London boy Danny knew a lot about hay. The pet shop man bought it in bales from the country, repacked it into polythene bags, and sold it to people who kept hamsters and guinea pigs and rabbits for fifty pence a bag. One bale of hay made dozens and dozens of fifty pence bags. They were piled up in a box in the corner of the shop. The pet shop man called the box his Gold Mine.

"Now, don't you think of buying that," he said when Danny wandered over to the Gold Mine. "I've a dozen bales in the back room that you can help yourself from. Got a rabbit at last?"

"No, I . . ."

"Guinea pig?"

"No . . ."

"Nothing wrong with hamsters!"

"I haven't a hamster either. I was just looking. I was wondering, how much would a whole bale cost?"

"There's about forty bags in a bale," said the pet shop man. "That's twenty pounds. Bagged."

"Oh," said Danny.

"What do you want a bale of hay for?"

"To make hay bags," explained Danny. "For

beds. In our camp. We're making an old-fashioned camp, Nathan and Anna and me in the garden of Paradise House."

"Three pounds a bale I paid for it, down in Kent," said the pet shop man. "I reckon you've bagged me up three pounds worth of hay, over and over! I'll drop you one off when I shut up tonight!"

Danny rushed back to Paradise House wild with excitement. Nathan and Anna, very hot and muddy, had just got the first paddling pool into place and were struggling with the second. Anna's mother had delivered it only minutes before.

"We keep having to take them back out to dig up stones," explained Anna. "They need something soft underneath."

"Hay!" said Danny triumphantly.

"What?"

"Hay! The pet shop man's given me a bale of hay . . ."

"*Given?*"

"Yes. He's dropping it off tonight. There'll be plenty for under the paddling pools, and we can stuff the rest into quilt covers for hay bags. I've got birdseed too."

"Brilliant!" said Nathan and Anna, and Danny looked very pleased. He was not usually the brilliant one.

They celebrated the bale of hay by filling the two new paddling pools with water and lying down in them. The water immediately

turned mud brown, so they filled them up again and added bubble bath. This made them look very clean and cool and good when their families arrived home for the evening.

"They have been no trouble at all," reported Miss Kent, smiling happily over their heads while Danny unpacked the paddling pool that his mother had just handed him. "Digging quietly for Vienna . . ."

"Vienna?" asked Nathan's father. "I wondered what those enormous earthworks were in the garden. They'd better get them tidied up before Old McDonald gets back! Anyway, why not Australia, like everyone else?"

"Vienna is Miss Kent's *worm*," explained Danny, and at once everyone lost interest and began drifting away. Danny remembered his birdseed and went back outside to spread it around the garden. He was just in time to meet the pet shop man before he knocked on the door. Where to hide the hay until they needed it was rather a problem. Every room in the house was full to bursting, and there was nowhere in the garden where it would not be seen.

"I know, Chloe's room!" said Nathan suddenly. "It will just fit in her cot!"

Nathan's father was decoyed out of the way while this was done, and when the bale of hay had been draped with Chloe's Teletubbies quilt and several pink towels it looked like it had been there for ever.

"Tomorrow," said Nathan, as they sat on the steps making plans at the end of the day, "we'll finish the stream . . ."

"Put down more birdseed and stuff the hay bags," said Danny.

"And what about the tent?" asked Anna "We'll need to have the tent tomorrow. It ought to be all ready, so that on Thursday morning, when Miss Kent gets up, there's her birthday camp waiting for her. How are we going to get the tent without her knowing?"

Nathan looked at Danny, and Danny looked

at Nathan. They had already discussed this problem.

"I got the hay," said Danny immediately. "And I'm doing the birds as well . . ."

"I'm doing the stream," said Nathan, just as quickly. "I worked it all out and I've done all the worst digging and it's nowhere near finished yet . . ."

"I've got Oscar to look after too, and all my worms too! I don't want them going wild just when they're starting to be tamed . . ."

"I shall have to guard Chole's room, now it's full of hay . . ."

"I'll have to go to the pet shop again tomorrow if I want more birdseed . . ."

"BUT WHAT ABOUT THE TENT?" demanded Anna.

"We thought you would like to do the tent," said Nathan.

"You know, find out where they keep it, and, er, and, er . . . What did we think, Danny?"

"Steal it," said Danny.

"Steal it?"

"*Borrow* it," said Nathan.

"Oh, *borrow* it," said Anna.

"Without asking, of course."

"I suppose," said Anna, after a long, long pause, "somebody has got to."

Chapter Four

Nothing went right on Wednesday morning. By nine o'clock the steps of Paradise House were too hot to sit on, the roses had wilted, and there did not seem to be a bird in the garden. Old Miss Kent was lying down in the dark with a headache.

"It's the weather," said her sister sympathetically.

"It's disappointment," said the Old Miss Kent. "I was so much looking forward to the next two weeks."

"I forgot about our holiday when I offered to look after the children," said the Young Miss Kent, as she had said a dozen times already that week.

"I know you did, dear!"

"And they have been very *good* children!"

"I know they have, dear!"

"It makes a nice change, I think, looking after them. We always go to the cottage!"

"Yes, always," agreed her sister, very sadly. "Oh dear!"

She did not say it made a nice change looking after the children instead. She got out her handkerchief and closed her eyes. The Young Miss Kent tiptoed away.

Anna found her in the kitchen. She was making a secret birthday cake, and if she had been making a secret bomb she could not have been more nervous.

"It is a cherry cake," she whispered to Anna, who was hanging round the flat with burglarous intentions. "She always had a cherry cake for her birthday, and I always had coffee and chocolate. Mixed. But this year she said No! No cake, she said. Seventy is too old for cake! ... Are you looking for something, dear? We keep the carpet sweeper

in there, and our winter coats . . ."

Feeling very guilty Anna shut the cupboard door that she had just pulled open.

". . . and Emily's tent," finished the Young Miss Kent.

Anna felt exactly like a burglar caught in the act but Miss Kent was too worried about her baking to take much notice. She had surrounded herself with bowls and basins and baking tins and three open cookery books. Each book had a different cherry cake recipe.

"Shall I help?" offered Anna, and was given the job of rolling cherries in flour, which Miss Kent said sometimes prevented them sinking and sometimes, sadly, didn't. From the Miss Kents' little sitting-room came the sound of sniffs.

Out in the garden Nathan and Danny were struggling with the stream. The ground was very hard.

"Why don't we soften it up with water?" suggested Danny, and before Nathan could stop him had turned on the hosepipe. Very soon paddling pools, lawn, and Nathan and Danny themselves were entirely covered in mud.

"Look what you've done!" said Nathan crossly.

Then they had an argument about hay. Nathan thought they should just fetch enough to line the paddling pool holes. Danny said they should bring the whole bale into the garden.

"It would just get soaked and dirty out here," said Nathan.

Ignoring Danny's protests he hurried inside, collected a kitchen knife, lowered the side of Chloe's cot and sawed through the tight orange strings that bound the bale. This was a big mistake. The hay was packed so tightly that the strings exploded apart. An avalanche of dead grass flowed onto the pale pink carpet. Chloe's cot vanished and became a haystack.

"I *told* you we should have opened it in the garden!" remarked Danny smugly. "I hope your mum doesn't suddenly come back for a visit! Why are you digging in it? You're making it worse!"

Nathan said that he was looking for the ends of the string, to tie it up again. Danny explained that this was impossible.

"They tie it up on the farms," he said. "Very strongly. With machines. Hay balers. Hay balers, hay balers, hay balers, I like saying hay balers! I expect your mum will go hairy-scarey sticking-on-the-ceiling bonkers!"

Nathan stopped trying to stuff the hay back into Chloe's cot and stuffed it down Danny's neck instead. There was a short fight. It ended when Danny slipped and landed on the hidden vegetable knife, slicing his knee, and Nathan cracked the back of his head on the doorknob.

"Don't bleed on the carpet!" ordered Nathan, rolling in agony.

"I'm not!" said Danny huffily, and hobbled outside to sulk.

After a while Nathan staggered after him with an armload of hay.

They lined the paddling pool holes in silence. Then they put in the paddling pools. Then they cut up Anna's old paddling pool and made the channels that were to join the three pools. Then they filled the whole thing with water and the bits of chopped up paddling pool floated out of their channels and onto the grass.

"Tiles!" ordered Nathan.

There were stacks of old roof tiles in one corner of the garden. They were left from the time when Danny and Anna had accidentally caused the roof of Paradise House to blow away. Nathan and Danny laid them flat, but overlapping, in the channels that joined the three pools. They made two tiled miniature waterfalls. Nathan cut his hand quite badly on the sharp edge of a broken tile but the waterfalls worked and suddenly the stream really was a stream, with water running in one end and out at the other.

"It works!" said Nathan triumphantly. "And it makes the right noise too!"

"And it waters the roses," said Danny. "It's perfect!" They grinned at each other, friends again.

"Crikey, it's hot!" said Nathan suddenly. "It's the hottest day yet!"

Danny nodded and looked up. The sky was not blue that day; it was the colour of dirty paint water. It made their eyes ache just to look at it. Their backs ached too, and their hands and their arms. They had not noticed while they were working how heavy the tiles had been, nor how much their cuts hurt.

"I'm stopping," said Nathan, and flopped down on the grass.

Danny turned the water in the hosepipe down so that it was hardly running at all and flopped down beside him.

Anna was not having a happy morning. The Young Miss Kent had said something that alarmed her very much. She said,

"I have never actually *made* a cherry cake before!"

"But you said she had one every year!" Anna had objected straight away. "You have chocolate and coffee, mixed, and she has cherry. You said!"

"Yes, yes," agreed the Young Miss Kent, hovering worriedly between her three different recipes. "But they make them at the cottage!"

"What cottage?" asked Anna, and Young

Miss Kent said, "Nothing, nothing! Take no notice! Go and cheer up Emily dear, there's a lamb!"

Anna went slowly out of the room, trying to think where the Miss Kents had been the summer before. She could not remember at all. What she did remember, more and more clearly, was the Old Miss Kent wringing her hands and asking, "But what about *our* plans?"

The Old Miss Kent was lying on the sofa with her eyes shut and a handkerchief over her nose. She seemed to be asleep. While Anna was watching she gave a little snore, sat up very quickly, and said,

"Goodness, dear! I was miles away!"

"I didn't mean to wake you up," said Anna.

"I dreamed I was in the countryside!"

Oh dear, oh dear, oh dear! thought Anna, feeling more and more certain that the Old Miss Kent *would* have been there, if her plans had not been upset by Young Miss Kent offering to look after them all.

"I've never been to the countryside,"

Anna said. She said it just for something to say, because she felt so awful, but it had an astonishing effect on the Old Miss Kent. She stopped mopping her face with the handkerchief and stared at Anna.

"Never been to the countryside!" she repeated.

"I've been *past* it," explained Anna. "On school trips and on the way to the sea. But we never stop and get out."

"That is quite dreadful!" exclaimed the Old Miss Kent, putting away her handkerchief and sitting up very brisk and straight. "Quite dreadful!" she repeated and before Anna could say a word she began talking and talking.

Into the stuffy little room she poured a jumble of pictures. Long grass and blackberries. Owls in the night. Stony paths on hills, and fossils in stones. A wobbling bridge over the pool in the stream. Little fish. Grasshoppers. Stiles in walls. Blue flowers called harebells. Stone circles and green mounds where Bronze Age men had made their homes four thousand years ago. It seemed that these were things that she felt Anna should know about. She stopped being old and sad and sorry for herself. She was sorry for Anna instead. She talked without pausing.

"Anna dear!" called the Young Miss Kent from the kitchen, and Anna stumbled out in a dream.

"I forgot the time!" exclaimed Young Miss Kent. "Take these, dear, and go and find the boys!"

She handed Anna the three lunch boxes that they had brought with them that morning. That was most unlike the Young Miss Kent. She usually liked to open them and arrange them on trays with sweets and jelly and other treats. Anna noticed that the birthday cake still wasn't in the oven and that there were now two more cookery books on the table. The Young Miss Kent looked very floury too, and there were cherries on the floor. Anna did not know if it would be more polite to pick them up or not to notice them. She picked them up, and that seemed from Miss Kent's face to be the wrong thing, so she put them back on the floor.

"Anna *dear!*" exclaimed the Young Miss Kent, and Anna hurried outside feeling worried.

Nathan and Danny were asleep in a bog. That was what it looked like to Anna, her head still full of the Old Miss Kent's countryside. A terrible mess of mud and plastic, soggy grass and dirty water.

"What are you *doing*?" she wailed, and they said very proudly that they had finished. They could not see what was wrong with their stream at all. Anna, repeating all that the Old Miss Kent had told her, said that it ought to sparkle and there should be plants growing all round and little fish in the deep bits. Nathan got very cross.

"Have you got the tent?" he asked sternly.

"Not yet."

"Well then!"

"My dinner has got all hot," remarked Danny, ignoring them both and examining his lunch box. "I hate melted sandwiches! And there's beetles in them!"

"There's beetles everywhere," said Nathan, and he was right. Minute black beetles with wriggling tails seemed to have appeared from nowhere.

"Thunder flies," said Danny, picking them off his sandwich. "It's no good moaning about the stream, Anna! It's not that bad, and anyway we haven't got time to do any more! Mum told Miss Kent I could go to the pet shop this afternoon and Nathan's got the hay bags to do . . ."

Nathan groaned. "I forgot about the hay! It's still all over Chloe's bedroom. You'll have to help me, Anna!"

"I've got to get the tent," objected Anna. "I know where it is. I'll have to see if I can sneak it out when the Miss Kents aren't looking . . . What was that?"

It was a sound like someone had punched a hole in a paper sky. It came again.

"Thunder?" asked Danny uncertainly.

"Thunder growls! And there's no lightning!"

"The sky's going brown!" said Anna suddenly.

"Perhaps I'd better go to the shop right now," said Danny jumping up. "I promised I'd tell Miss Kent before I went and she'll never let me out if a thunderstorm has started! I'll go straight away! One of you had better turn the hosepipe off!"

"I will in a minute," said Nathan. Anna had given him an idea, with her talk about fish in the stream. Oscar, Danny's goldfish, lived in a round glass bowl. If Oscar in his bowl were stood in one of the pools, thought Nathan, the glass would hardly show at all. Only Oscar would show. It would look like he lived there.

All Nathan intended to do was try it. Just for a minute. If it looked good, he thought, they would ask Danny if Oscar could stay there, and if it looked silly, no one would know. When Anna was back indoors and Danny was on his way to the pet shop he fetched Oscar in his bowl from Danny's bedroom. He lowered the bowl very carefully into the top pool, which was the cleanest. Oscar swam straight over the top and disappeared.

It was the worst thunderstorm any of them

had ever known. Danny came back from the pet shop just in time. A moment later it was pouring with rain. Lightning flashed pink and purple and blazing white and the thunder shook the roof.

"Thank goodness you're back!" exclaimed the Old Miss Kent, who had been waiting on the doorstep for him. "Anna is playing with Nathan! Go and join them Danny. My sister is a little upset! Unless you are frightened of the storm too?"

"I think it's lovely!" said Danny.

He found Anna in Chloe's bedroom but she was on her own. Nathan, she told Danny, had looked scared stiff when he was fetched in. The moment the Old Miss Kent had gone away he had disappeared.

"Hiding," said Anna as they stuffed armloads of smothering hay into duvet covers and watched the rain stream down the window. The Young Miss Kent was crying, she went on to say, the tent was still in the kitchen cupboard and the cherry cake was in the bin.

"It sank," she explained. "It looked like a nobbly burnt pizza . . . Oh!"

Paradise House shook under another crack of thunder.

"It's just noise," said Danny reassuringly. "It can't hurt you."

"I'm not scared," said Anna, "I'm *not* scared! But I would be if I wasn't! I wonder where Nathan is."

Nathan was in the garden. He had remembered to turn off the hosepipe, but the stream still ran like a brown river, in at the top and out at the bottom and overflowing into the rose bushes. He was crouched at the bottom end, desperately hoping to catch Oscar before he was swept away. He was as wet as a river himself. Above him the storm seemed to be tearing the sky apart and flinging the pieces at his head. The lightning switched on and off like the end of the world and the thunder sounded like falling stones, but Nathan stayed where he was. He thought if he was struck by lightning at least he wouldn't have to face Danny and tell him what he had done.

Gradually the storm moved away. The rain ended. The stream stopped running. Nathan searched the pools one last time and then slowly went indoors.

"I don't care what it is about!" said Danny's mother angrily. "I don't care *what* it is about! Don't you ever, ever, ever behave like that again!"

The grown-ups were home. Danny's mother had come back just in time to see Danny, soaking wet, launch himself on Nathan, also soaking wet, and knock him to the ground. They had searched in vain for Oscar.

"I'll get you another one," Nathan had offered, and Danny had gone mad.

Nathan's father was the next one home.

"I don't care whose hay it is!" he roared. "You will clear up every blade, *every blade*, if it takes you all summer!"

Anna's mother, knowing that Danny and Nathan had both been sent to bed in disgrace, hardly dared to ask if Anna had been good.

The Miss Kents said she had been no trouble at all. They very nobly did not add that she had been caught red-handed sneaking out of their flat with their tent. Anna, hot-faced and guilty, could hardly look at them. She did not have to be sent to bed. She went herself.

Chapter Five

The Young Miss Kent woke up the following morning feeling astonishingly cheerful. It was five o'clock. The room was full of sunshine and the air was as clear and cool as country air. She crept into the kitchen and in no time at all, and with no recipe book, she whisked together a cherry cake that rose like golden foam.

Anna also woke very early. At first she couldn't think why she felt so bad. Then she remembered the ruined birthday camp, and stealing the tent, and the Miss Kents who she suspected ought to be getting ready to go on holiday in the country. Probably they would be if she had not moaned so much about the holiday club. Then she remembered Oscar, lost in the storm. The moment she thought of Oscar she forgot everything else and climbed out of bed. Nathan and Danny had said Oscar must be dead, stranded among the roses. She thought she would try to find him before Danny came down.

All the mud from the digging had been washed away by the storm, and the grass was green and clean again. Birds were everywhere. They had found Danny's birdseed at last. The roses smelt wonderful.

In the night the muddy water had cleared in the paddling pools. The earth had settled in patterns like waves all over the blue bottoms. The water sparkled. In the last pool Oscar was swimming among the weed from his goldfish bowl. He looked very happy and very alive. Anna turned on the hosepipe, just a little, so that the water ran over the tiled waterfalls.

"It needs plants," she thought suddenly.

Her mother grew plants in pots, ferns and leafy plants. For the next half hour Anna crept in and out of Paradise House, and when she had finished the stream looked like a real stream, with plants hanging over and a real little fish. In between trips to the house she threw handfuls of earth at Nathan and Danny's bedroom windows, and at last they woke up.

Danny looked out and saw sparkling water and Anna waving and jumping and pointing excitedly to the bottom pool. A minute later he was in the garden too, and then Nathan was beside him.

"It's beautiful," said Anna.

Danny said, "Let's go back in and clear up the hay."

They did this as silent as mice, filling three quilt covers before Nathan's father woke up and caught them. "Well I never!" he said, and got out the vacuum cleaner quite cheerfully.

The Old Miss Kent woke up and sniffed and said, "Cherry cake!" out loud and got out of bed.

The Young Miss Kent was already dressed. She said "Yes, cherry cake, Happy Birthday,

dear. Get dressed very quickly!"

"Are you all right?" asked the Old Miss Kent.

"Get dressed *very quickly*!" repeated the Young Miss Kent, handing her a cup of tea and disappearing.

It's beautiful

The Old Miss Kent thought perhaps her sister was ill and began to get dressed very quickly indeed.

"There's three hay bags outside the front

door," said the Young Miss Kent, popping back in again for a second.

"*Three hay bags?*"

"Hurry up! Come outside!"

"Real hay bags?" asked the Old Miss Kent, but she was not allowed to look at them for more than a moment. She was towed outside.

"They've made a stream," said the Young Miss Kent. "With plants hanging over, and a fish. Look! And they've put down birdseed for the birds. And they made hay bags. No wonder Anna wanted the tent. They've made you a birthday camp!"

When Nathan and Danny and Anna, dressed and breakfasted, came back into the garden the tent was almost up. The Old Miss Kent was tightening guy ropes while the Young Miss Kent stuffed in the last of the hay bags. They said it was the best birthday camp they had ever had, and they said that Danny and Nathan and Anna were the cleverest, kindest children they had ever known.

"I don't know about that," said Nathan's father, when the Miss Kents, Young and Old, had been dragged off by the children to test the hay bags, "but I do think there should be a party tonight! A proper old fashioned one! Hot dogs and banana splits like I used to have!"

"Jelly and trifle and ice cream and jam tarts," said Danny's mother.

"What else?" asked Anna's mother. "What to drink?"

"Let's make a list," suggested Anna's dad, and they listed lemonade and ginger beer, jelly, ice cream, jam tarts and trifle, cold chicken and ham and sausages on sticks, and hot dogs and banana splits to please Nathan's dad who said it would not be a party without them. Then they divided the list between them and hurried off to work, forgetting to pack up their children's lunches.

"What shall we do?" asked Anna at lunchtime.

"Telephone for pizzas," said the Old Miss

Kent, who was getting younger by the minute.

The birthday party was at suppertime, and all the parents came, as well as Chloe and Nathan's grandad, Tiger, Jake, Rover and Pluto. Also a worm who looked very much like Vienna. It went on very late. The grown-ups stayed talking together long after Danny, Nathan and Anna had collapsed onto the hay bags, worn out with food and party games. It was far into the night when the Young Miss Kent whispered, "Good night, Vienna!" and went happily to bed.

The talking went on the next day too, and there was a lot of telephoning as well, and the day after that the Miss Kents left for their country holiday after all. They took with them their tent and the Paradise House children and Nathan's father who said he was tired of waiting for Next Year. Nathan's father and the Miss Kents stayed at the cottage, but the children slept in the tent on hay bags. There were owls in the night and fossils in stones and a stream at the bottom of the damson orchard.

It didn't rain once all summer.